DungeonWorld

#1: One Hot Spark
#2: The Big Whiff
#3: Bang the War Drum
#4: The Royal Mess
#5: The Ghoul Ranch

DUNGEON WORLD

E. DANIEL JAMES

THE ROYAL MESS

This is a work of fiction. Names, characters, places, and incidents either are the product of the author's imagination or are use fictitiously. Any resemblance to actual persons, living or dead, events, or locales is entirely coincidental.

Copyright © 2022 by E. Daniel James

All rights reserved. No part of this book may be reproduced or used in any manner without written permission of the copyright owner except for the use of quotations in a book review.

First paperback edition 2022
Book Illustrations by Michelle Nobles
ISBN 978-1-957349-06-0 (paperback)
ISBN 978-1-957349-07-7 (ebook)
Honest Carpenter Publishing
Visit the author online!
www.edanieljames.com

THE ROYAL MESS

E. Daniel James
Illustrated by Michelle Nobles

1. The Queen's Invitation

LIFE IN DUNGEONWORLD is funny.
One moment, you're about to be blasted out of a huge cannon. The next moment, you're riding in a golden carriage on your way to meet the Queen.

It's enough to make a guy's head spin!

I turned to Thoracks, the huge blue ogre in the carriage with me.

"Explain to me again why I'm not pudding mush right now."

Thoracks sighed.

"I already told you…the Queen heard about that little caper you pulled in the Army. She issued a Royal Order that you were to be brought to the Palace immediately. And when the Queen gives an order, you *follow* it."

"Okay, fine," I said. "But why me?"

Thoracks gave a weary shake of his head.

"I can't imagine what the Queen wants with a scrawny brunt like you."

A scrawny brunt like me…

I was starting to wonder if there even was another brunt like me.

See, there are a lot of us human servants in Dungeonworld. Unlucky kids who got snatched by monsters and brought to this weird underground kingdom. The ogres, goblins, and trolls who run the place call us brunts because they make us do the "brunt" of the work.

But the thing is, most brunts don't cause half the problems I do!

See, I've got this way about me…

Wherever I go, *trouble follows*.

It doesn't help that I've got a bit of a temper. And it doesn't help that I sometimes get bored and have to make things more exciting. And it *definitely* doesn't help that I hate following orders.

That was where my last job went wrong...

Thoracks is pretty much my boss down here. A couple of weeks back, he'd shipped me off to be a drummer boy in the Dungeonworld Army.

I tried to do my duties like I was supposed to.

Honest!

But then I got into a little spat with a nasty goblin named Lubwort. We had to settle our problems in a duel. So, I sort of stole this magic drum and used it on him, and... well, let's just say the outcome wasn't pretty.

Imagine a thousand hairy, greasy

monsters slow-dancing romantically!
Ugghh.
I still couldn't get the image out of my head.
Anyways, the Army brass was going to shoot me out of a huge cannon for punishment. But, at the last second, Thoracks came galloping in with a message that the Queen of Dungeonworld wanted to see me.
Just like that, I was rescued!
Or so I thought...

The carriage bounced and rumbled up the rocky road.
"What did you mean I might have been better off with the cannon?" I asked.
Thoracks turned one of his yellowish eyes on me.
"I meant it like I said it," he replied. "On a scale of what's more dangerous—a thunderous cannon or the Queen of Dungeonworld—the cannon doesn't even rank!"

I rolled my eyes.

"Come on. She can't be *that* bad."

Thoracks scoffed.

"Wanna bet? Around these parts, her temper tantrums are downright legendary. Folks call her by a nickname...*The Royal Mess*. But they'd never say it to her face, mind you. If you did that, even your shadow wouldn't know what became of you!"

I chewed a thumbnail, suddenly worried. Thoracks reached a paw into his leather shirt and pulled out a change purse. He went poking through it with a clawed finger.

"They put her face on the doink," he said.

"The *what?*"

"The doink. Here, take a look..."

He handed me a little copper coin like a penny. I peered at it closely. The coin showed the face of a little gobliness looking sideways. Even on a tiny, worn-out piece of metal, she seemed pretty angry.

"Huh. So, that's Queen Esme...Malfa..."

"Queen Esmerelda Malfuza Tippy Von Scumbert," Thoracks said. "And don't you forget it!"

He plucked the coin from my fingers.
"How'd she become Queen?" I asked.

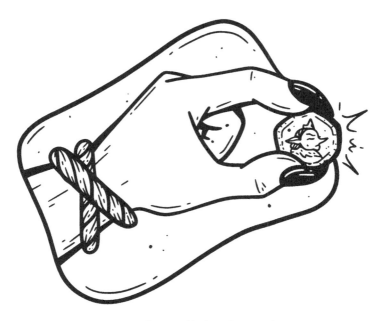

"Same way they all do down here," Thoracks said. "She crushed her enemies. Vanquished her critics. Seized power with an iron fist. The usual rigamarole."

I gulped.

Now I was *definitely* worried.

Thoracks turned his huge horned head towards me.

"Look, I'll give you some advice. Be a

perfect gentleman around the Queen. Never speak unless she speaks first. And no matter what, *don't play the joker*! The Queen hates when someone steals the spotlight from her. Got it?"

I nodded rigidly.

"G-got it."

A little goblin in silk crimson-and-gold clothes had been riding on the side of the carriage since we'd left the Army base. He suddenly cried out in his shrill voice.

"Approaching the Royal Palace!"

Thoracks sat up straighter in his seat.

"Get ready to put your manners on," he said.

I tried to quiet the butterflies rampaging in my stomach.

The Palace awaited!

2. The Royal Palace

I GAZED OUT THROUGH the carriage window.

For the moment, we were still trundling along the typical Dungeonworld roads. I saw stone walls rising up in the darkness around us. Torches flickering in iron brackets. Bats swooping and looping in the gloom.

That's Dungeonworld for you. An endless hollowed-out cave full of bridges, rocks, and bottomless pits. Nothing glamorous. But when we turned down a gravel lane, I got my first glimpse of how royalty lives down here.

"Wowza!"

I'd never seen anything like it!

We passed through a tall iron gate into an immaculate courtyard. Thorny hedgerows grew all around us in an elaborate maze. Stone fountains spouted arching jets of water, and green peacocks strutted about preening their feathers.

Horns announced our arrival.

Toot-Tootle-Tooot!

The carriage whipped around a circular driveway lined with fires glowing in golden braziers. The little goblin escort leaped down from the side of the carriage. He opened the door and gave me a fancy bow.

"Step out, please, sire."

I climbed down out of the carriage.

Thoracks lumbered out after me.

I took one look up at the palace and let out a whistle.

"This place looks like a castle!" I said.

Thoracks elbowed me.

"It *is* a castle, dunderhead."

The building reminded me of fairy tale palaces I had seen in books.

It was made of carved white stone, and it seemed to have a hundred pillars, columns, and turrets. Gargoyles and cherubs decorated all the nooks and crannies. Bright torchlight shone through the crystal-clear windows.

A dozen Royal Guards stood before a sweeping staircase at the Palace entrance. Their silvery armor sparkled, and their sharpened spears shimmered. The little goblin gave a flourishing wave.

"Welcome to the palace of Queen Von Scumbert! I trust your journey was quite comfortable?"

I gave a little shrug.

"I guess it wasn't too bad."

"We always aim to please," the goblin said with a toothy grin. He turned and gave a sharp snap of his fingers.

"Now, cuff the prisoner!"

Guards came clanking forward quickly.

I jumped back.

"Wait...*prisoner?*" I said.

The little goblin lifted his chin.

"You are here at the Queen's request," he said. "But until she has determined your fate, you will be a prisoner at her mercy. As such, you shall remain in chains."

One of the silver-suited guards gave me a gruff sneer. I didn't think these guys were going to let me off the hook. So, I held out my hands, and he slapped golden shackles around my wrists.

Click!

"Take him to the Queen!" the little goblin shouted.

The guard put a heavy hand on my shoulder. The other guards surrounded me. Together, they began marching me up the Palace stairs. Thoracks followed along anxiously several paces behind.

What have I gotten myself into? I thought.

We entered the Palace in a loud, clanking column. As nervous as I was, I couldn't help gawking at the place!

The courtyard and entrance were

nothing compared to the inner chambers. We walked across marble floors that were slick enough to bowl on. The walls were jam-packed with gold-framed paintings and velvet curtains. Armless statues and jumbo vases lurked in every corner.

We approached a set of doors shaped like a giant keyhole. Trolls in crimson tunics stood at the entrance.

"Prepare to meet the Queen!" they barked.

With surprisingly graceful motions for monsters the size of dump trucks, they pulled the doors open and bowed. The guards thrust me forward.

We walked into the nicest room I'd ever seen! Everything in here was pink and gold. Polished wooden furniture lined the walls, and a great crystal chandelier hung from the lofty ceiling. On a platform at the center of the room stood a fabulous golden throne...

And on that throne sat a tiny gobliness.

Queen Esmerelda Malfuza Tippy Von Scumbert.

She was wearing a dainty crown of gold and diamonds. Her pink silk dress was covered with a hundred sparkling baubles and jewels. In her right hand, she held a skinny wand with a little silver fist on the end.

She rose to her feet and looked down at me over her sharp, beaky nose.

"So...you're the one they call *Spark*."

3. Rough Audition

I wasn't sure how to respond…
Yes sounded too casual.
Yes, your majesty just sounded weird.
I was thinking of trying something like, *Yes, Queen Von Scumbert*. But before I could get it out, one of the silver-suited guards jabbed me with the butt of his spear.
"Answer the Queen!"
"Oww!"
I rubbed the spot on my leg where he'd poked me.
"Yeah," I grumbled. "That's me."
She curled one of her wispy eyebrows.
"And you're the one who played the

enchanted drum and caused my soldiers to—how did they put it—*dance around like a bunch of half-witted ninnies?*"

I wasn't waiting to get jabbed again.

"Yeah. That was me too," I said.

The Queen cocked her head.

"I see..."

She glared at me with her beady, green eyes for a moment. Then she turned to a golden bowl sitting on a little table to her right. She jabbed a razor-sharp fingernail into the bowl. It came back out with a cinnamon-covered cockroach speared on the tip.

She popped it into her mouth.

Crunch!

I pulled my head back in disgust.

The Queen inspected her needle-like fingernail. Then she folded her hands in her lap and pinned me once more with a penetrating glare.

"Normally, I would have you whipped and trounced for tampering with my soldiers. But on this particular occasion, I must say I found your ruse to be quite *funny*. In fact, I believe I laughed for a good ten seconds or more."

I waited to see if she was kidding...

She wasn't.

The Queen shifted on her velvet throne and continued.

"My last Royal Jester suffered a rather horrible accident. I find myself in need of a new one. I thought a brunt of your wit and talent just might do the trick."

"You want me to be your *jester*?" I asked.

Apparently, this question was out of line too because the guard jabbed me again with his spear.

"Do not ask questions of the Queen!"

"*Ouch!*"

I winced and ground my teeth.

The thermometer in my head went up a few degrees...

"That depends, young man," the Queen said haughtily. "I've summoned you here to see if you truly have the talent I require. I thought an audition might be in order."

She clapped her little hands.

"Go on. Do something funny!"

I lowered my eyes.

"You want me to just...be funny?"

"Of course! That's what jesters do, is it not?"

How should I know what jesters do? I thought.

In the human world, we don't have jesters. We have comedians. And I'm definitely not one of them! But I got the feeling that disagreeing with the Queen in her own Palace would be a bad idea. So, I racked my brain.

Come on, Spark. Be funny!

What sort of joke do you tell a queen, though? I tried to recall the one my grandfather once told me about the pirate with the brown pants. But it took me a while to piece it together, and eventually, the guard decided I had taken too long.

He jabbed me once more with the spear.

"Answer the Queen!"

The thermometer in my head spiked.

"Poke me with that spear again, and you'll be talking out of your ear," I muttered.

He hissed through the slits in his silver helmet.

"What did you say, prisoner?"

"You heard me, you walking tea kettle."

His eyes flared widely.

"You'll pay for that!"

He drew his spear back to give me the hardest poke yet. But at the last moment, I leaped back, and he stabbed it right down onto the other guard's foot.

"YEEOOWW!"

The injured ogre jumped into the air, clutching his toes.

I scoffed.

"That's pretty good aim" I said. "Want to try again with your eyes open?"

"Blasphemous brat!"

The guard swung the spear like a baseball bat. I ducked, and he whacked a third guard right on the shiny forehead.

Crong!

"OOF!"

Now two guards were staggering around in pain. I took the opportunity to trip the one with the bruised toes. He fell to the floor with a sound like pots and pans banging around.

Clang! Clong!

The first guard stalked me in a crouch.

"Surrender yourself, brunt!"

"Why? So you can punish me? Grow a brain!"

He dropped the spear and came at me with his bare hands. I ducked and dodged. I faked and feinted. He chased me around like a cat chasing a mouse. Guards all over the hall began leaping into the fray.

"Grab that ruddy brunt!" a troll shouted.

In the confusion, I picked up the forgotten spear and brandished it wildly. I was ready to take on all comers!

But before they could close in around me, a shrill screech brought everything to a halt.

"Waaait!"

The Queen had leaped up from her throne. She was waving her stumpy arms around. I thought she was going to issue an angry order, like, *Off with his head!* But to my surprise, she didn't seem angry at all.

In fact...she was *laughing*.

Tears of mirth were streaming down her face. Her chubby chin was wobbling with pleasure. She clasped her hands together joyously.

"Yes!" she said. "That's exactly what I need! *Royal comedy!* You'll do just fine!"

I gave her a look of disbelief.

"Wait a sec? Are you telling me...?"

"That's right, young man. You're hired!"

4. Clean-up Job

IT TOOK A while for things to calm down after that.

The silver-suited guards were helped to their feet. Spears and swords were returned to their owners. The light-footed goblin ushered me to the Queen's throne with Thoracks tagging along behind us, bewildered.

The Queen was gazing at me with lustrous eyes.

"Thoracks, why have you been hiding this gem from me!"

"Uhh, well, your majesty," Thoracks said. "We might not have realized exactly what kind of gem we had on our hands."

"A diamond in the rough," the Queen said. "That's what kind!"

She looked at me like I was the most fantastic person she had ever seen. But as she gave me a closer inspection, a wrinkle appeared in the center of her green forehead. She tisked disapprovingly.

"You're simply filthy, though," she said. "When did you last bathe?"

Honestly, I couldn't remember the last time I'd had a bath.

"Ehh...it's been a while."

"You shall take a luxurious bath," the Queen said. "Then, you shall be dressed in the finest attire. Once you are squeaky clean and presentable, you will join me tonight for a Royal Banquet in your honor!"

A banquet in my honor? Just a few hours ago, I'd been sitting in a musty prison cell. I felt like I'd wandered into some weird dream!

"Thank you...your majesty," I mumbled.

The Queen batted her eyelids girlishly.

"Please," she said. "Call me Tippy."

I might have blushed a little.

"Take my new Jester to the Royal Baths!"

the Queen said.

The light-footed goblin sprang forward. He bowed so low he nearly kissed his own toes.

"Right this way, sire…"

I followed him across the great hall towards the keyhole doorway. Just before we left the room, I turned to see Thoracks gawking at me. It looked like he'd been clubbed on the head by a troll!

The little goblin led me through room after magnificent room on our way through the Palace. My head was whipping in every direction as we wandered beneath arches and dome-shaped ceilings. We arrived at a set of steamy glass doors.

"The Royal Baths, sire."

He pulled the doors open. A cloud of warm, foggy air rolled out. I stepped inside and almost had to shield my eyes.

"Holy moly!"

This place was the size of a gymnasium! It was made entirely of white marble. There were pools and hot tubs and fountains everywhere I turned.

Fluffy towels sat piled up on golden benches, and white robes hung from silver hooks on the wall. Trays full of fancy soaps, shampoo bottles, and sponges lined the edges of the tubs.

The little goblin pranced ahead of me. He selected a clam-shaped tub at the center of the room and turned the tap. Steaming hot water gushed from the faucet.

Splooosh!

"Would the Royal Jester like bubbles?" the goblin asked.

I shrugged.

"Why not?"

He spun another knob. Jets of ivory soap spurted into the water from swan-shaped spouts. The tub immediately began to foam and froth. A smell like an ocean breeze wafted up to my nose.

The little goblin gestured around the tub.
"Sir has soaps, sponges, and towels aplenty. Shall he be needing anything else?"
"I think I'm good," I said.
"Excellent. The Royal Bath is yours."
He swept out of the room and pulled the doors shut.
I stood there looking at the spacious tub.

I almost got a little bit dizzy from the warmth and sweet smells.

Back in the human world, I'd never been all that crazy about taking baths. But after days spent working in blacksmith shops, sewers, and dirty fortresses, the idea of a hot bath was pretty dang close to heaven.

I didn't even bother stripping off my dirty clothes. I took a running leap from the edge of the tub and...

"Cannonball!"

SPLASH!

I surfaced in a cloud of foam and bubbles.

"Ahhh..."

I took a few laps around the tub doing

backstrokes. The warm water licked my sides. The layer of crusty dirt and sweat slowly melted away from my skin. I leaned against the marble wall and hooked my elbows over the edge of the tub.

"Now, this is living!" I said.

I spent a good, long while trying out all the fancy soaps and shampoos. I rubbed myself with loofahs and sponges until my skin was glowing pink. Then I got out, dried myself with about a dozen towels, and put on a thick, soft robe.

I walked through the glass doors whistling a tune. The little goblin was waiting in the hallway.

"Was the gentleman's bath satisfactory?"

"Not too shabby," I said.

"Excellent! Let us now visit the Haberdashery."

"The Habba-*what?*"

"The Royal Tailor, sire. You must look capital for the Queen's banquet!"

I twisted my head.

"Lead the way!"

5. A Fancy Occasion

WE PASSED THROUGH more exquisite rooms and halls, my bare feet squeaking on the marble floors. I left a flowery scent in my wake.

We entered a wood-paneled room that smelled like fresh leather and shoe polish. Shelves held huge bolts of cloth, and mirrors stood in every corner. A sharp-looking ghoul with a pencil behind his ear approached us.

"Welcome to the Palace Haberdashery. How may I be of service?"

The little goblin lifted his chin.

"The Royal Jester is in need of fine attire for a banquet this evening."

The ghoul's eggy eyes lit up.

"Wonderful! We are only too eager to please, sire. And what style of attire would the gentlemen wish for?"

I turned to the light-footed goblin.

"What should I wear?" I asked.

"It is entirely up to you, sire. But let me give you a word of advice. The Royal Jester should always dress in his own unique idiom."

I squinted at him

"My own idiom, huh?"

I wasn't too sure what idiom meant. But I thought I got the gist of it. They wanted to see a bit of my personality. The rare old Spark!

Okay, I thought. Let's see here...

I folded my arms and inspected the room.

"Let's start with some of that neon orange cloth over there," I said.

"Fantastic choice, sire!"

The ghoul tailor went to work. He knelt in front of me with pins held between his cracked lips. His scabby hands stitched and snipped and tucked. He used a cloth tape to pull measurements.

I watched my outfit take form.

"Can we get some lightning bolts down the side here?"

"Right away, sire!"

When he was finished, he stepped back.

"Well," he said. "What do you think?"

I posed in front of a mirror, admiring myself at different angles. My costume had puffs and pleats. Cuffs and collars. Loops and lapels. My hat looked like a slightly deflated pumpkin.

"I look awesome!" I said.

The little goblin brushed a tiny bit of fluff from my sleeve.

"And are you ready to join the banquet, sire?"

My stomach gave a mighty grumble. I hadn't had a proper meal in days.

"Sure thing," I said. "I'm starving."

"Then you are in for a treat! The Queen keeps a splendid table. When you dine at the Palace, you really dine at the Palace."

I pointed a finger through the door.

"Take me to the food!"

The Banquet Hall made all the other rooms look tiny!

The rafters were so high you could have flown a plane beneath them. A long table stretched most of the way across the room. It was covered with a silk table cloth and a bazillion plates, glasses, forks, spoons, and bowls.

Dozens of finely-dressed ghouls, goblins, and ogres were already seated. They began whispering behind their hands the moment we entered the room.

"Is that a brunt in the Queen's Palace?"

"What in Griswold's name is he wearing?!"

"I've never seen such a hideous outfit!"

I suddenly felt much less confident about my choice of clothing. I considered doing a quick about-face out of there. But before I could make up my mind, the Queen called me down from the head of the table.

"There he is, my Royal Jester!"

She patted a seat next to hers.

"Come! You shall dine in my place of honor."

I crept down to the end of the table, a hundred eyes on me. The Queen took one look at me up close and clasped her hands to her chest.

"Oh, you look simply smashing! Such bravado, such flare! Tell me, were the lightning bolts of your own invention?"

"Uh, yeah. Just a little idea I had."

"A stroke of brilliance!" the Queen said.

She snapped her fingers.

"Seat my Jester at once!"

A troll in a tunic lumbered forward and pulled a chair out for me. I slipped into it, feeling a little more confident.

I looked down the long table at the faces of all the fancy monsters seated there. To my surprise, I saw Thoracks halfway down! He was wearing what looked like an ugly red tuxedo. I tried giving him a friendly nod, but he seemed stiff and nervous.

"Let the dinner commence!" the Queen screeched.

Now servants and waiters rushed forward from the wings of the room and set a bevy of silver platters and tureens down on the table. They lifted the platter lids to reveal a delicious feast!

A ghoul gently tied a napkin around my neck.

"Tonight, sire, we serve jellied peacock eggs, cream of python soup, moose brains, and blobfish soufflé. What would the Royal Jester wish for?"

I sat there running the options through my head.

Honestly, they all sounded disgusting. But I'd learned that food in Dungeonworld was usually better than it sounded. And since I was in the Palace, I figured it had to be twice as good.

"Why don't I try a bit of everything?" I said.

"A wise decision, sire."

The meal came to me on a dozen little plates and saucers. I slurped the python soup, munched the moose brains, and gobbled the blobfish.

The Queen watched me attentively.

"Is everything satisfactory, my sweet?" she asked.

"Fantastic!" I said.

I looked around the table, chomping on my meal. The banquet guests seemed to be stately, royal ogres and goblins of various sorts. They looked like they were used to fine things and high society.

"Who are all these people anyway?" I asked.

"Attendants of my court," the Queen said.

"So, what? They just...hang around the Palace?"

"Yes, I suppose so. What do you think of them?"

I thought about giving her a polite

response. But the Queen seemed to like it best when I spoke straight from the heart. So, I shrugged and made a face.

"They seem sort of stuffy to me."

"The Royal Court is *very* stuffy," she said. "That's why I've brought you here. To liven things up a bit!"

She gave me a penetrating stare as she said this. It took me a moment to realize that she was issuing a direct order.

"Like, right now?" I asked.

"It is your job, you know," the Queen said.

I could tell she was used to getting exactly what she wanted. And I had a feeling that there would be consequences if I didn't live up to my share of the bargain. So, I looked around the room.

Right, I thought. *Liven things up a bit...*

I observed the long table spread with half-empty platters and dishes. I took note of the haughty guests drinking wine with their pinkies up, and the troll servants standing by the wall.

An idea began to form in my mind.

"All right," I told her. "Watch this..."

6. Dinner Pranks

I snapped my fingers angrily.

"Waiter! Come here!"

One of the tunic-wearing trolls leaped forward.

"Yes, sire?"

I picked up one of the dainty saucers in front of me.

"This jellied peacock egg is undercooked. Send it back to the kitchen."

"Right away, sire."

The troll took the tiny plate in his rocky hands. He turned around carefully, balancing the jellied egg as it wobbled and wiggled. But before he could walk away, I tucked a bit of the

tablecloth into the golden belt on his tunic.
 He got three booming steps...
 Then the whole banquet began to slide.
 Clish! Clash! Clink!

Dishes, glasses, and silverware began to topple over and tumble as the troll dragged the tablecloth like a tail. A hunk of moose brains lurched off its platter and rolled into the lap of a fancy ogress.

Splat!

"Oh, my dress!" she shouted.

Glasses of wine spilled. Dinner rolls rolled. A row of silver candlesticks tipped over and set fire to a bunch of dried-up purple flowers.

Whoosh!

As you could have guessed, madness followed.

The fancy guests jumped to their feet. But they were packed in so tightly at the table that there was nowhere to go. Feet got tangled. Chairs flipped over. Heads bonked together.

Meanwhile, the witless troll just kept right on trudging towards the kitchen. Dishes spilled off the end of the table in a waterfall of fine china. Food splattered and splurted onto everything.

The guests wept and wailed.

"I've ruined my white gloves!"

"Cream of python soup right down my trousers…"

"My diamond earring fell in the soufflé!"

The Queen, however, clapped her hands joyously.

"Fantastic!" she said. "Oh, simply fantastic!"

She laughed maniacally.

And I laughed too.

This is pretty good work on short notice!

She looked at me with one of her adoring stares.

"Oh, Spark. I knew you were special. Par excellence!"

I took a moment to pat myself on the back.

The other waiters had finally managed to stop the troll. They were struggling to untuck the tablecloth from his belt. Meanwhile, a dozen ghouls began to comfort the guests and hastily scoop the fallen food from their laps.

The Queen rose from her chair.

"Tonight, you sleep in the Imperial Guest Suite. It is the finest in the Palace!"

"Are you sure?" I asked.

"Of course! Nothing is too good for my Jester!"

She looped her arm around mine.

"Come! You have earned your rest..."

We began to sweep across the Banquet Hall arm-in-arm. I looked back once to admire the mess I had made. Amidst the goblins and ogres mopping moose brains off their fancy clothes, I saw Thoracks standing there.

His face was as red as his tuxedo. He gave me an angry scowl.

My guess was that he hadn't liked my performance too much. But hey, I was only doing what I was told! I flashed a smile back in his direction. Then, I continued onward.

Ta-ta!

That night, as promised, I slept in the Imperial Suite. The Queen wasn't kidding. This place was fit for a king!

The wood-carved bed was the size of a wrestling ring. It was piled deep with silk sheets, blankets, and enough throw pillows to fill a dumpster. A courtly ghoul butler was there to attend to my every need. He folded his white gloves behind his back.

"Would sire like anything before bed?"

I scratched my chin.

"Got any candy around here?"

"Of course, sire! Would you like cinnamon-covered cockroaches? Sugary cotton cobwebs? Or honey-drizzled lizard legs?"

I considered it for a moment.

"Why not all three?"

"Capital notion, sire."

He brought me a silver platter with nearly fifty pounds of sweets on it! I lay buried under covers, munching away to my heart's content. Violin music drifted through the Palace halls.

"Not bad for a guy who was in shackles this morning," I said.

I ate candy until my stomach felt like it would burst. Then, I just rolled over and went right to sleep.

7. High Life Hijinks

IN THE MORNING, there was a knock at the door to the Imperial Suite. I swam up from a deep, drowsy sleep. My head hurt from all the sugar I'd eaten.

"Oo' is it?" I grumbled.

"The Royal Valet, sire!"

"Fine. Come in…"

The little goblin came prancing into the room and gave me a bow.

"The Queen sends her compliments, sire. She wishes to know if you would like to accompany her for breakfast in the Royal Gardens?"

Really, all I wanted to do was roll over in

my covers and go back to sleep. But when the Queen says come, *you come!* So, I slid out of bed.

"Hang on. Let me get my Jester suit…"

The little goblin led me through the back doors of the Palace onto a large pavilion that overlooked a sweeping lawn. Down below, gardeners were busy trimming bushes and watering flowers.

"What a view!" I said.

The blooming flowers were the size of trumpets. There were bushes shaped like mythical animals, all trimmed to perfection. Bees the size of birds zipped around, pollinating things.

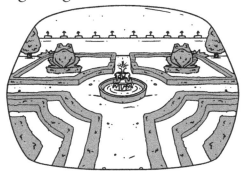

The Royal Mess

The Queen was sitting at a little table on the pavilion.

"There you are, my sweet!" she said. "Come, fill your belly. We have mildew pancakes, plump boar sausages, and freshly squeezed beetle juice."

I parked myself across from her at the table and tied a napkin around my neck. A ghoul waiter held up a crystal jug full of golden liquid.

"Hemlock syrup, sire?"

"Pour it on," I told him.

He soaked my pancakes until they were mushy. Then, I picked up a fork and started devouring the breakfast.

I hadn't eaten this good since I had first shown up in Dungeonworld! As I munched, the Queen watched me with her red lips puckered in a smile.

"I simply can't stop thinking about your little performance last night," she said. "It was *fantastique*! You have such a flair for the dramatic."

I blushed, munching a boar sausage.

"Mmm, thanks," I said. "I guess it wasn't

too bad."

"Tell me, where did you learn it from?"

I gave a little shrug.

"I suppose I'm just a natural-born troublemaker."

"You're an *artiste*!" the Queen said. "My last Jester was such a *bore*. He insisted on telling jokes, blowing horns, juggling. He lacked your brilliant vision!"

She swept a hand over the lawns.

"Take these gardens, for instance. Why, I bet you could make them more exciting in the blink of an eye!"

I looked out over the bushes and flowers in the distance. I really didn't see any *reason* to make them more exciting. They looked pretty nice as they were. But I could feel the Queen's gaze boring into me...

"Well, then?" she said.

I looked down at my unfinished pancakes. They'd be cold and soggy if I left them now. But I figured there was no avoiding it. I took off my napkin, put down my fork, and got up slowly from the table.

"Uh…I'll be right back."

The Queen smirked and crossed her arms.

I climbed down a staircase and crept into the bushes near the flower beds. I set up camp here and gazed around the garden, looking for some inspiration.

"Come on, Spark," I said. "Flex the old mischief muscles…"

I saw a ghoul watering a big bed of rose-gold flowers nearby. Behind him, a goblin was pitchforking dung straight from a cart while a sleepy mule dozed between the traces. I rubbed my chin thoughtfully.

I think I can work with this...

I got down on all fours and went crawling through the flowers.

I found the long hose that the ghoul was using lying in the dirt. I poked my head up to see if the Queen was watching. She gave me a knowing smirk from the pavilion. So, I grabbed the hose, twisted it, and put a big kink in the line...

The water spouting from the end turned to a trickle.

"What the...?"

The ghoul looked down the nozzle.

I let the kink out of the hose.

A gush of water shot into his face.

Sploosh.

"Aggghhghgh!"

The ghoul flailed backward, sputtering.

I thought that would be the end of it. But the ghoul bumped straight into the goblin unloading dung. The goblin tumbled forward, and the prongs of his pitchfork jabbed the mule in the rear end.

Heee-haaaw!
The mule bolted!
It took the cart with it, dung and all, and went rampaging through the gardens. It cut right through the carefully planted flower beds, churning up petals and clods of dirt. It smashed through a bush shaped like a sea serpent.
"Grab him! Grab him!"

Ghoul gardeners everywhere leaped to their feet and gave chase. They slipped in the dung spilling from the cart and toppled over each other in the flower beds.

I just sat there, dumbfounded.

I honestly hadn't expected it to go so far! Even now, the mule was mowing down a bush shaped like a rhinoceros. I suddenly felt guilty about messing up so many hours of hard work. But the Queen seemed to feel differently.

She jumped up and down on the pavilion, clapping her tiny hands.

"Oh, extraordinary! Bravo! Such wit!"

I came out from behind the bush, scratching my arm.

"That worked pretty well," I said sheepishly.

"You have outdone yourself!" she said.

She waved me towards her. I had no choice but to climb the pavilion stairs.

"Oh, my sweet Spark! There's never been such a prankster! How did I get through life without you?"

How does anybody get through life with *you?* I wondered.

"Come, come!" she said. "Let us retire to the inner chambers."

Behind us, the gardeners had finally managed to bring the cart to a stop. They were gazing in astonishment at the ransacked garden and the piles of dung that lay scattered everywhere. The whole place was in ruins.

I felt like a bottom-feeding slug as I strolled back into the palace with the Queen.

8. The Pit of Discomfort

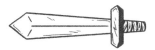

THE QUEEN LED me into the great hall. She was still gloating over my accomplishments. But when she got a good look at me in the Palace lights, her face soured into a little frown.

"Oh, but you're simply filthy now," she pouted.

I looked down at myself. My hands and knees were smeared with mud from crawling in the gardens. I even had a little dung on my new jester suit.

The Queen made a shooing gesture.

"Go!" she said. "Take a bath. We shall rejoin later for more fun."

She swept off down the hall, her long nose held high. I watched her go with a sense of relief. I turned and started to head for the Royal Baths, but a voice nearby startled me.

"Pssst...Spark!"

I glanced over to find Thoracks hiding behind a bush. He looked ridiculous. He was still wearing his goofy tuxedo from the night before, and he couldn't even hide his bulk behind the twiggy branches. An elephant would have drawn less attention.

"What are you doing?" I whispered.

"Trying to get a word with you alone!" he hissed.

I took a long look up and down the hall.

"Well, I don't see anybody else," I said.

Thoracks glanced around

suspiciously.

"The Palace has a lot of ears," he said. "Get in here."

He waved me over urgently with a big, blue paw. I rolled my eyes but squeezed in beside him. We stood there in the little space behind the bush awkwardly. He gazed at me in my Jester suit.

"You seem to be enjoying yourself, I see."

I gave a little shrug.

"It's not so bad here, I guess."

"Maybe for *you* it ain't," Thoracks said.

I cocked my head.

"What's that supposed to mean?"

"It means a lot of decent folks are having to clean up your messes!" he hissed.

I fidgeted.

"Come on. Those were just little pranks."

"*Little* my left hoof! Waiters are still scrubbing python soup out of the Banquet Hall carpet. And it'll take months to get the Royal Gardens back into shape!"

I felt my cheeks redden a bit.

"Look, I'm just doing my job!" I said. "Besides, the Queen loves my pranks. As far as she's concerned, I'm the bee's knees."

"That's the other thing I wanted to talk to you about…"

He pulled me further behind the bush.

"The Queen's just tickled pink with you now," he said. "But she's got a habit of turning on folks lickety-split. And when she does…well, let's just say bad things happen to them."

I looked at him sideways.

"What *sort* of bad things?"

Thoracks' eyes flittered furtively.

"I ought not to even be showing you this," he said. "But follow me…"

He slipped out from behind the bush and went creeping down the hall on his clunky hooves. I thought about just ignoring him. But I was too curious now. I ducked out of the bush and followed along.

We tiptoed through the Palace like a couple of thieves.

"Where are we going?" I hissed.

"Shhh! Just stay close."

He crept up to a statue of a troll fighting a wolf in a corner of the hallway. Very carefully, he jiggled one of the wolf's fangs. A wooden panel in the wall began to swing open noiselessly.

"Woooah," I whispered.

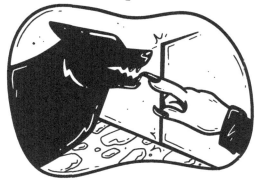

Thoracks walked through the dark doorway that had opened.

"Get in!" he said.

I stepped into the secret compartment and pushed the wooden panel shut behind us. I looked around to find that we were standing at the top of a stone staircase. Torches burned in brackets on the wall. A cold draft blew up from below.

"Is this a secret passageway?" I asked.

"Yeah, Palace is full of them. Stay close to me."

Together, we crept to the bottom of the stairs. Then Thoracks began guiding me through a series of hallways. It was like a maze down here! I would have gotten lost in an instant if I were alone.

"How do you know so much about the Palace?" I asked.

"I used to be a soldier in the Queen's Guard," Thoracks said. "I spent a right good amount of time roaming these halls."

"Really? I didn't know that."

"Ha! What you don't know would fill a troll's trousers…hold tight here. Don't go no further."

He stopped me at an intersection of hallways. Very carefully, he waved me forward and pointed around the corner.

"Peek down there," he whispered.

I craned my neck out and peered around the corner. A long, dark hallway led to an iron door at the end of the hall. A wooden sign hanging above the door read: PIT OF DISCOMFORT.

"Pit of Discomfort?" I said quietly. "What's that?"

"That's where you wind up if the Queen gets tired of you," Thoracks said. "She sends you down to see *The Royal Pain*."

"And who's The Royal Pain?"

"The Queen's Tormentor," Thoracks hissed. "He's a maniac! His only job is to think up terrible things to do to folks. The Pit of Discomfort is his office, if you want to call it that."

I looked at the scary iron door.

"What's it like in there?" I asked.

Thoracks' eyes got big.

"Nobody knows. Because nobody's ever gone down there and come back up."

A little chill went down my spine.

I was leaning forward for a better look when, suddenly, the iron door swung open. A tall figure in a black robe emerged through the doorway. He slammed the door shut behind him and began walking straight toward us.

Thoracks put a big paw on my shoulder and pulled me back into the shadows.

"Quiet!" he whispered in my ear.

The figure went stomping right by us, his boots echoing in the stone hallway. He seemed to be on urgent business. He didn't even notice us cowering in the corner. Eventually, his bootsteps faded in the distance.

"That was him!" Thoracks wheezed.

"He's a tough-looking customer," I said.

"You bet your bippy he is. Nasty as a two-tongued cobra."

He tugged on my shoulder.

"Come on. Let's get out of here."

We slipped back down the hall, quiet as mice.

9. A Bad Decision

BACK IN THE glowing splendor of the Palace, the creepiness of the basement began to wear off a little bit. But I was still in a bad mood.

"Why did we even bother going down there?" I asked.

"I wanted you to see what you were dealing with," Thoracks replied. "I thought it would help you make your decision."

"Oh? And what decision is that?"

Thoracks clenched his big paws nervously.

"Look, I think bringing you here might have been a bad idea. If I were you, I'd consider

slipping off while you still have the chance."
"What? Like, run away?"
"Precisely!" Thoracks said.
I waited to see if he was kidding.
His bullish face was completely serious.

I laughed.
"Come on. I can't just disappear!"
"Sure, you can!" he replied. "Just slip out the door. Duck through the window. Shimmy down the gutter. Vanish like a fart in a

windstorm! The Queen will forget about you in time."

"Where would I even go?" I asked.

"Anywhere!" Thoracks said. "Anywhere but here. I've got a bad feeling about this whole arrangement. I think the sooner you're gone, the better."

I looked at the elegant hallways around me. I thought about the mountain of candy waiting in my bedroom.

"But...what if I don't want to leave all of this?" I said. "I mean, let's be honest. I've got a pretty good thing going here. All the fancy food I can eat. My own private spa. A bed the size of a launchpad. Compared to everything else in Dungeonworld, this is the life!"

Thoracks' face darkened.

"I reckon you'll like it a whole lot less when you're hanging by your thumbs!"

I waved the idea away like a pesky fly.

"Come on. That's not going to happen to me."

"Oh yeah? Tell that to the last Royal Jester."

I looked at him mistrustfully.

"The last Royal Jester?"

"That's right. You remember how the Queen said he'd suffered an accident? Well, that's one way of putting it. Another way is to say that she sent him down to the Pit of Discomfort!"

My eyes bulged.

"You kidding me?"

"Not hardly..."

I squinted at him, trying to call his bluff.

"I don't know," I said. "Seems sort of fishy to me."

His blue face turned red.

"Fishy?"

"Yeah, fishy. You're just now telling this to me? I'm starting to think that you don't want me here for another reason. A selfish reason."

"Oh? And, pray tell, what might that be?"

"You're jealous!" I said.

"Jealous? Of a brunt like you?!"

"That's right," I said. "You've been bossing me around ever since I showed up in Dungeonworld. Sending me from one crummy job to the next. Now, I'm the Queen's favorite person. And I think you just can't stand it!"

His eyebrows climbed up to his horns.

"You've got some nerve," he said. "I always knew you were a hot-headed, obnoxious little squirt...but I never took you for a danged fool!"

We stood there glowering at one another.

Thoracks spoke in a growl.

"Look, I'm leaving the Palace," he said. "And if I were you, I'd be doing the same in a jiffy. But I don't expect that to get through your thick, tiny skull!"

He turned and began stomping off down the hallway.

For a moment, I considered following him.

Sure, Thoracks had been a pain in my

butt the whole time I'd been in Dungeonworld. And sure, he bossed me around a lot. But he had saved me from that cannon. And sometimes, we even got along a little bit.

I dithered there, weighing it up in my mind.

But I hesitated too long.

Thoracks turned the corner up ahead. In an instant, he was gone. And with him went my last good piece of common sense.

Ahh, let him go! I thought. I've got more important things to do. I turned around and stalked off in the other direction.

I was almost to the Royal Baths when a voice startled me.

"There you are, my sweet!"

I turned to see the Queen bustling up the hallway in her pink dress. I wasn't sure why, but my stomach gave a frightened lurch. She zoomed up and gave me a disapproving look.

"Why, you're still filthy! Haven't you bathed yet?"

I looked down at my mucky suit.

"Uhh, I got a little held up," I said.

The Queen clucked her tongue.

"Tisk, tisk! But there's no time now. You'll have to do without…"

"Why? What's the big rush?"

"We have a special occasion," the Queen replied. "This afternoon, you and I are to preside over the Royal High Court!"

I was getting used to seeing the word Royal in front of pretty much everything around here. But so far, I hadn't heard any mention of a High Court.

"Okay, how does that work?" I asked.

"Well, ever so often, I hear the cases of law-breaking in my Palace. I act as judge and jury, handing down sentences. It is one of my noble duties. And now, I'm appointing you my Royal Counsel. You shall pass judgments with me!"

I blinked my heavy eyelids.

"You're putting me on the High Court?"

"Of course!" she said. "The Queen can do whatever she wants, you know."

She pinched my cheek.

"Come! We must go to the High Court Chambers."

I didn't like the sound of this.

But I also didn't really have a choice. The Queen took my hand and began dragging me down the hall, her pink dress rustling. I was starting to wonder if I should have slipped off with Thoracks when I had the chance.

But it was too late now.

10. Courtly Business

TWO GUARD TROLLS were stationed outside the doors to the High Court. When they saw us approaching, they tapped their spears on the floor loudly and pulled the doors open.

"Make way for the Queen!"

We walked into a dark, gloomy room. The walls and floors were black marble. Fires burned in braziers on the wall. A high podium sat at the far end of the room.

The Queen guided me across the floor.

"Come, my sweet. Let's get seated."

We climbed a little set of stairs to the top of the podium. I found two pillow-topped seats at the peak. The Queen sat on one cushion. I took the one next to her, feeling as awkward as ever.

I had a dizzying view from up here.

Looking across the dark room, I saw more silver-suited guards lining the walls. Standing in the corner by himself was a tall figure in a dark robe. My heart almost seized up when I recognized him.

It was the Royal Pain!

This must have been the place he was rushing off to. He looked scarier than ever looming over there by himself. His face was completely hidden beneath his dark hood.

The Queen banged a gavel on her podium.

Clack! Clack!

"High Court is now in session," she screeched. "Bring forth the offenders!"

The door opened once again.

A guard troll trooped in a bunch of miserable goblins, ghouls, and ogres. The prisoners were wearing rags and shackles. It looked like they'd been sleeping on cold floors lately. Just behind them, the little goblin valet followed along, holding a scroll.

The troll thumped his spear.

"Halt!"

The group clanked to a stop.

The little goblin valet pranced forward. He made a quick, snooty inspection of the prisoners. Then he spun around and addressed the Queen in a loud voice.

"Your Majesty, these subjects before you are guilty of terrible crimes committed against the Queen and her property! Shall I read the offenses?"

The Queen flicked her fingers impatiently.

"Yes, yes. Proceed…"

The little goblin unfurled the scroll with a flick of his wrist. Pointing to a lady ogre wearing an apron, he read from the parchment.

"Subject A, the ogress Brumhilda. Guilty

of dropping ten eggs while preparing an omelet in the Royal Kitchen."

The Queen scoffed.

"Wasteful!" she said.

I shifted uncomfortably on my pillow.

I had broken about a hundred peacock eggs when I'd trashed the Banquet Hall yesterday! It seemed silly to charge somebody with egg-breaking when I was sitting right here. But the trial continued nonetheless.

The little goblin pointed to a hunch-backed ghoul.

"Subject B, the ghoul known as Pumice. Guilty of driving horses recklessly down the Queen's streets."

The ghoul spoke up desperately.

"I was rushing to fix the gardens, your highness!"

But the troll jabbed him with a spear.
"Silence, prisoner!"
Pumice lowered his oozy head.
Now I really began to sweat. Poor Pumice must have been coming to clean up the mess I'd made in the Royal Gardens that morning. His punishment was totally my fault! I thought about speaking up, but the little goblin continued right along.

"And finally, your Highness, a most grievous offender…Subject C…the goblin called Snort."

I sat up in my seat.

This prisoner was barely older than I was! He was practically trembling beneath the Queen's gaze. The little goblin valet put extra venom in his words as he read Snort's crime.

"Guilty of *stealing*, your Highness…"

"Stealing?" the Queen said.

"That's right!" the little goblin cried. "Stealing a piece of candy!"

The Queen gasped.

"Of all the diabolical, despicable acts!"

I couldn't believe what I was hearing…

I had fallen asleep in an actual pile of

candy just last night, and no one had batted an eye. I probably still had ten pieces stuck in my underwear! But poor Snort was facing punishment for stealing one little piece?

It didn't make any sense!

The Queen was in a terrible rage nonetheless.

"I should be glad you brought me only *three*," she said. "I simply could not stomach news of any more crimes! And to think, they were all carried out under my Royal nose."

The little goblin snapped up his scroll.

"The subjects await your judgment, Highness…"

The Queen tapped the gavel on her palm. Her nasty lips narrowed.

"Let's see, then. Shall I have them dragged through thorn fields by stallions? Buried in ant hills while slathered with honey? Or shall I hand them over to *The Royal Pain*?"

At the mere mention of the Tormentor, the subjects began to shake.

The Queen turned to me.

"What do you think, my sweet? What shall I choose?"

My spine went slack.

"*Me?* Choose?"

"That's right. You are my High Counsel now!"

I couldn't believe this. She wanted me to pass judgment on these poor ogres and goblins? As if I had behaved any better than them since I'd first shown up at the Palace!

I looked down at the pitiful subjects quaking below me. They were begging me for mercy with their eyes. In fact, the whole room was watching me now. I knew I had to make a decision soon.

I gave a nervous shrug.

"I don't know," I said. "Why don't we just take it easy on them?"

The Queen's eyelids narrowed.

"What was that?" she said. "Take it *easy* on them?"

I swallowed with a dry throat.

"Sure," I said. "Maybe we could…you know…just let them go?"

The sickly, sweet smile remained on the Queen's face. For a moment, I almost thought she would agree with me. But then the gavel cracked quietly in her scrawny hands.

Snap…

That's when I knew I was in trouble.

11. The Royal Pain

The Queen sprang to her feet. "You think I should take it *easy* on them?!"

I waved my hands innocently.

"I'm just saying...maybe what they did wasn't so bad, you know?"

I was trying to make her see reason. But a fire had been lit inside her twisted little brain, and it was starting to get hotter and hotter.

"These imbeciles destroy my property... rampage upon my roads...pilfer my pantry...and you want me to take it *easy on them?!*"

My eyes trailed to the ground.

"It was just a thought..."

She towered over me on her little pillow. "You claim to be my loyal subject, then you question me in my own High Court? Why, you're just like all the rest of the sniveling scum in my kingdom...deceitful and treacherous!"

She flung her half-broken gavel at my head.

"Imbecile!"

I barely ducked in time to avoid it. When I looked back up, she was aiming a razor-sharp fingernail at my nose. Her voice rose to an ear-splitting shriek.

"You want me to take it *easy* on them, do you? Fine! If you wish, I shall set them all free... and *you* shall receive their punishments instead. How do you like that?!"

My eyes opened wide.

"*Me?*"

"That's right. It's either you or them. Which will it be?"

I couldn't believe how quickly the tables had turned! I looked down at the shivering prisoners below me. They seemed so pitiful in their rags. They were all gazing up at me hopefully, begging me with their eyes.

I felt hot panic roll through my body.

There was no way I could let them get punished for a bunch of silly little offenses. Not when I'd been running wild since the minute I had shown up at the Palace! I had to do the right thing...

"Fine," I mumbled. "I'll take their punishments."

A bitter smile spread across the Queen's green face.

"Then you have sealed your fate."

She snapped her fingers.

"Release this rabble!"

The guard troll threw open the door.

"Leave the Queen's Court at once!"

The prisoners bowed hastily and began clanking through the door in their shackles. They seemed too terrified to say another word. But the young goblin, Snort, turned once and gave me a smile of gratitude. I somehow managed a queasy smile back.

Then the Queen turned her scorching gaze upon me again.

"As for you," she said. "You have a date with The Royal Pain."

She gave one swish of her finger.

"Send forth my High Tormentor!"

The black-robed Royal Pain stepped forward from his place in the corner. The other guards gave him space as he marched slowly across the room. He stopped at the foot of the podium and turned his shadowy face towards me.

"Come..."

I let out a weary breath.

"Hang on," I said. "I'll be right down."

I climbed down slowly from my seat. When I reached the ground, the Royal Pain put a massive, green hand on my shoulder. He spun me around to face the Queen.

She was gazing down at me from the high podium with her lips curled in a vicious sneer.

"You will *rue* the day you showed up at my Palace," she said.

I gave her a dry look.

"Too late, Tippy."

She screeched with anger.

"Take this brunt to the Pit of Discomfort!"

"Yes, your Majesty..."

The Tormentor bowed. Then he turned me around and began shoving me across the room. The silver-suited guards stood back nervously to let us pass. As we walked through the doors, a very annoying thought occurred to me.

Thoracks was right...I should have left when I had the chance!

―✺―

The Tormentor led me slowly through the Palace. It was a shameful walk. I had to see all of the places where I had caused so much trouble.

Ghouls were still scrubbing the carpet in the Banquet Hall. Beyond the expansive windows, gardeners were tossing ruined flowers onto a heap.

Definitely not my finest chapter in

Dungeonworld.

But I didn't want it all to end now!

I gave a nervous laugh.

"Any chance you might just give me a slap on the wrist?" I said.

The Royal Pain shoved me forward.

"Many," he said.

Total backfire!

We reached the statue of the troll and the wolf. The Tormentor pulled the trick fang, and the hidden panel opened in the wall. Cold, dank air wafted up from below. The Royal Pain gave me another hard shove.

"Go on."

Hot fear began to course through my body.

I looked down the long, stone staircase. I knew that if I went down there, I'd probably never come back up again. I'd be totally forgotten. Somehow, that didn't seem like a fitting end for a guy like me.

So, I spun around.

"No," I said.

The Tormentor's hood darkened.

"You dare defy me?"

"Pffft! A guy wearing a bed sheet? You bet. You look like the kid who forgot his Halloween costume and had to make one at the last second."

I heard him gasp within his hood.

"I'll squash you where you stand!"

I lifted my chin.

"Do your worst, you walking laundry bag!"

The Royal Pain drew back his huge, green hand. I tensed every muscle in my body. I figured my only hope was to knock him down the stairs and make a break for it. I mean, I'd rather go out fighting than grovel like a wimp!

But just when I was about to spring, a loud metallic thump rang through the stone hallways.

CRONG!

The Royal Pain dropped to the floor like a sack of spuds. Another dark figure rose up behind him.

12. The Dung Cart

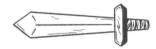

It was Thoracks.

"What are you doing here?!" I said.

"What's it look like?" he replied. "Saving your skinny butt once again."

He was holding a heavy metal skillet, the kind you fry eggs in. That was what he had used to clonk the Royal Pain. I almost laughed.

"A frying pan? *Seriously?*"

"It's all I could find

on short notice!" Thoracks said. "I had to sneak back in through the Royal Kitchens. I didn't assume you'd be so choosy."

"I'm not," I said. "It's just…I'm surprised to see you."

His eyes trailed to the side.

"I heard on my way out that the Queen had taken you to a High Court session. So, I hung around outside just to see what would happen. When I heard you'd pardoned those prisoners…well, I couldn't just leave you here to rot."

I'd never been so grateful in my life.

"Thank you," I said.

"Hmph. You're welcome."

We stood there looking at the rumpled shape of the Royal Pain lying on the ground. His hood had fallen back, revealing a goofy-looking ogre's face. He had tiny ears, a big nose, and a weak chin. No wonder he wore a hood!

"What if someone finds out what you did?" I asked.

"The Queen thinks I'm already gone," Thoracks said. "I reckon she'll assume you whacked him on the head and gave him the slip. Fits your record, anyways."

"Good point," I told him. "So, what do we do next?"

"Get you out of the Palace in a hurry. Come on!"

He set off clopping down the hall on his hooves. With a burst of excitement in my chest, I ran along after him.

Thoracks led me through a series of lavish halls, then down some curving stairs. We slipped through a small side door on the bottom floor and popped out near the Royal Gardens.

I'd never been so relieved to smell musty Dungeonworld air!

"This way," Thoracks said. "Stay low!"

We went scampering across the back lawns, dodging behind bushes. As we ran, I looked straight into the castle windows above us. It was still calm in there. Nobody seemed to have yet noticed that anything was amiss.

"Where are we going?" I whispered.

"The Royal Stables," Thoracks hissed. "We need a ride out of here."

We skirted along the edge of the Gardens and made our way down to a large stone building. It was shaped like a fancy barn. We entered through a back door, and—*wham*—a hot, stinky odor wafted over us.

It reeked of cow poop in here!

Ghoul horses were sticking their heads out of rows of stalls. They watched us as we hustled down the aisle towards a door at the far end.

Thoracks stopped and looked around.

"We need to keep you hidden until we're far away from the castle," he said.

"Okay...how?"

He pointed across the room.

"With that!"

The dung cart that had gone rampaging through the gardens was standing by the large stable doors. The sleepy mule was still standing in the traces. Flies were buzzing all around it.

"We're going to ride the mule?" I asked.

"I'm going to *drive* the mule," Thoracks said. "You're riding in the back."

"What...in the poop?!"

"It's the only way to keep you hidden!" Thoracks said. "If someone stops us on the road, I'll say I just borrowed the cart. They won't think to look inside."

My stomach turned over as I stared at the steaming pile of horse dung in the back of the cart. I put a hand over my mouth.

"I don't know about this," I said.

But just then, horns began blowing outside. We heard angry voices shouting near the Palace. It seemed that the guards had finally discovered the Royal Pain.

Thoracks gave me an impatient look.

"Care to wait for the search party?"

"Fat chance," I grumbled.

"Then hop in!"

Reluctantly, I climbed into the back of the cart and lowered myself into the horse dung.

It was warm and steamy, and it reeked to high heavens! Thoracks shoved me in deeper with his huge mitts.

"Lay down," he said. "I'll cover you up."

"But wait! How am I going to breathe?"

"Just lay down, would you!"

I did as I was told.

The hot mush wallowed up around me. Thoracks ran across the barn and took a pitchfork down from the wall. Hastily, he started scooping more loads of dung over me.

In a matter of moments, I was completely buried! I heard Thoracks' muffled voice come through the pile.

"I'm opening the barn doors. Hold tight!"

There was a creak of hinges. Then the cart lurched and jerked as Thoracks climbed into the front.

"Stay quiet," he hissed. "We've got guards up ahead!"

My heart suddenly began beating faster. I clenched my eyes shut.

The wheels bumped and rattled as we began to roll forward slowly. We pulled out into the main courtyard, and I felt Thoracks aim us for the front gates. But before we could get too far, loud ogre voices shouted up ahead.

"Thoracks, you still here? We thought you'd gone already."

"I'm just leaving now, lads."

"Oh yeah? What's with the dung cart then?"

"Uhh...thought I'd haul away some filth for the Queen."

There was a heavy pause.

I thought for sure we were cooked!

The guards were muttering back and forth. But before they could make up their minds to investigate, more horns began blaring up at the castle. I could hear feet stamping in the distance.

The guards called back hastily.

"Go on then, mate. The Queen is in a right huff. Seems that scrub of a Jester gave the Royal Pain a whack! He's loose in the Palace now. We're goin' in to help sniff him out."

"Well, thump him on the noggin' once

for me, would you?" Thoracks called.
"Righty-o!"
Thoracks lashed the mule.
"Yaaah!"

I could feel the cart picking up speed now as we bounced down the path, away from the treacherous Palace. Warm dung pressed in on me from all sides. I could barely breathe from the poop fumes!

As I lay there in the stinky darkness, a ridiculous thought occurred to me.

I arrived here in a golden carriage...and now I'm leaving in a dung cart.

That's Dungeonworld for you!

THE END

Made in the USA
Las Vegas, NV
23 May 2023

72446939R00069